Little Ant's Valentine

S.M.R. Saia

Illustrations by Tina Perko

It was almost Valentine's Day. All the ants in the anthill were planning what they wanted to do for the ant that was the most special to them. Every year on Valentine's Day, the ants exchanged sweet treats and sweet words. But no one had ever given a sweet treat or a sweet word to Little Ant.

These were the kinds of things that the girls in the anthill said about Little Ant: Little Ant is stuck up! Little Ant doesn't share! Little Ant likes to be alone too much! I hope Little Ant doesn't try to give a valentine to me!

"I hate Valentine's Day," Little Ant sulked. He knew that no one wanted him for a valentine, and no one thought that he was special. So while the other ants made plans and hid surprises, Little Ant spent all day, every day, working alone.

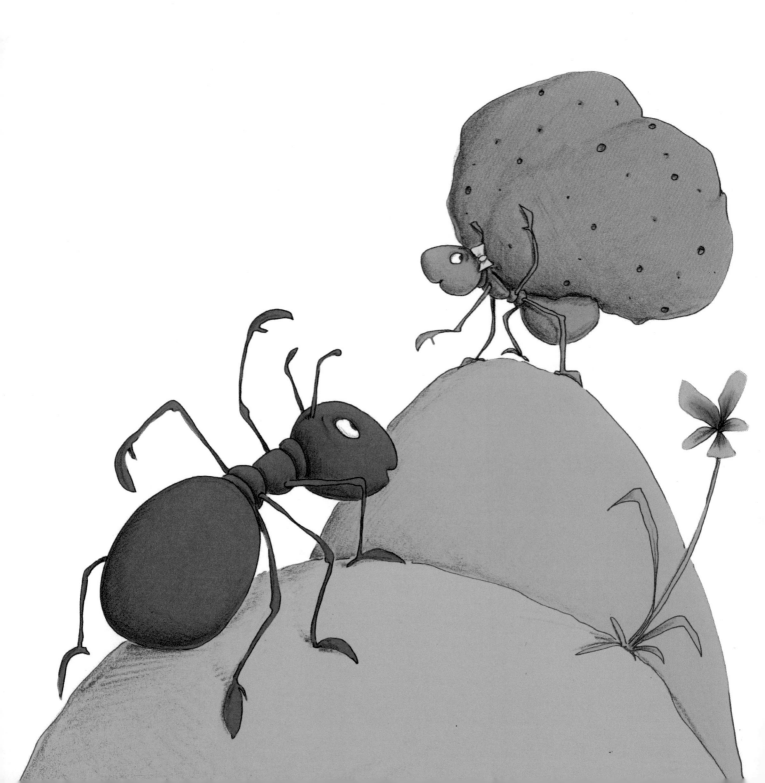

One afternoon he was away from the anthill, looking for food and laying down a trail behind him, when he crossed paths with an ant that he did not know. She was such a pretty ant that Little Ant stopped in his tracks just to look at her. She looked strong and smart and quick, and the crumb on her back had to be at least fifty times her body weight.

"What do you want?" the pretty ant demanded. Little Ant was tongue-tied. He had never seen such a pretty ant before.

"I am Little Ant," he said at last.

The pretty ant barely glanced at him as she walked past. "Well good for you," she said. "I am busy, and you should be too. I do not have time to talk to strange ants from other anthills!"

Little Ant stared after her. When he could no longer see her, he set back about his work, but all he could think about was the pretty ant. Every time he saw a crumb, or a seed, or a morsel on the ground, he wondered what the pretty ant would think of it. He imagined carrying each one back to her anthill for her, and wondered what it would be like to see her smile.

Little Ant hoped to see the pretty ant again. "I am not always friendly," Little Ant thought to himself. "But I am still a good ant. I am strong and smart and quick. I can lift fifty times my body weight. I will talk to the pretty ant again, and this time she will talk to me."

But when Little Ant saw the pretty ant again, she was just as rude as she had been the day before.

"Why are you so mean to me?" Little Ant asked her. This time, the pretty ant stopped.

"All the ants in my anthill say that I am stuck-up," the pretty ant said. "They say that I don't share. They think I like to be alone too much. No one wants to give a valentine to me. So why should I be nice!"

"I know just how you feel," Little Ant said.

"Leave me alone," the pretty ant said, and she turned away.

But Little Ant didn't want to leave her alone. "That pretty ant is a lot like me," Little Ant thought to himself when she was gone. "I wish that someone liked me just like I am. I wish that someone wanted to give me a valentine." Little Ant wasn't thinking about how much he hated Valentine's Day. He wasn't sulking that no one wanted him for a valentine. "I am going to give a valentine to the pretty ant," Little Ant decided.

For the next several days, Little Ant looked for the perfect sweet treat. He tried to think of the perfect sweet words. He went farther from his anthill than he had ever gone. After a while, Little Ant began to see some promising things on the ground. Humans had been here, and there had been a party. Excited, he ran from sweet to sweet, in search of the perfect valentine for the pretty ant.

Should he give her a jelly bean?

Should he give her a gumdrop?

Should he give her a peppermint?

Nothing Little Ant found seemed just right. Everything was sweet and delicious, but they were all...ordinary. And the pretty ant was not ordinary.

Just as he was about to give up with disappointment, Little Ant stepped around a large stone and there, to his astonishment, he found the perfect valentine. He took a quick nibble at one edge to confirm that it was sweet and delicious. It was big. It said everything that he felt in his heart. And it was not ordinary.

Little Ant hoisted the valentine onto his back. It tested his strength to lift. It also tested his courage. "Maybe the pretty ant doesn't want a valentine from me," Little Ant worried. Maybe she would say that she was too busy to accept a valentine. Maybe she would tell Little Ant to leave her alone again. "I don't care," Little Ant said to himself. "I like the pretty ant, and I want to give her a valentine."

And on Valentine's Day, that is exactly what he did.

The pretty ant was surprised. "Why do you want to give a valentine to me?" she asked. "I am stuck-up, and sometimes I don't share, and sometimes I like to be alone too much."

"That does not mean that you don't deserve a valentine," Little Ant said.

"Thank you, Little Ant," the pretty ant said. She smiled, and Little Ant felt all light and happy inside. He felt better than he did when he found the biggest and tastiest crumbs. He felt better than when he lifted fifty times his body weight.

"I'm not so grumpy when I'm with you," the pretty ant said shyly.

"It's much easier to be nice when you feel like someone likes you," Little Ant agreed.

Published by Shelf Space Books
ISBN: 978-1-945713-18-7

Made in the USA
Middletown, DE
17 January 2019